KENNY ROGERS presents

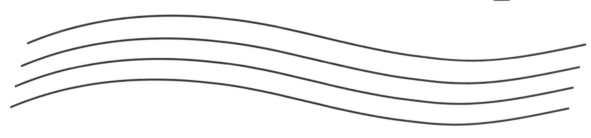

THE **GREATEST**

Based on a song
written by Don Schlitz

ADDAX
PUBLISHING
GROUP

Published by Addax Publishing Group Inc.
Copyright © 2000 by Kenny Rogers
Lyrics copyright 1999 New Hayes Music (ASCAP)/New Don Songs (ASCAP)
All rights administered by New Hayes Music (ASCAP) All Rights Reserved International
Copyright Reserved Used By Permission

Bob Snodgrass
Publisher

Jerry Hirt
Art Direction/Design

An Beard
Managing Editor

Michelle Washington
Publicity

ISBN: 1-886110-91-3

Printed in the USA

1 3 5 7 9 10 8 6 4 2

ATTENTION SCHOOLS AND BUSINESSES
Addax Publishing Group Inc. books are available at quantity discounts
with bulk purchase for education, business, or sales promotional use.
For information, please write to:
Special Sales Department, Addax Publishing Group
8643 Hauser Drive, Suite 235, Lenexa, KS 66215

Library of Congress Cataloging-in-Publication Data is on file at the Library of Congress

A special thanks to Jim Mazza and Dreamcatcher Entertainment,
Brian P. Hakan and Associates, Paul Zamek, Jim McGuire, Misti Filipiak, Claire Cook,
Kelly Junkermann, Shaun Silva, Eli Bishop and Rawlings Sporting Goods.

KENNY ROGERS presents

THE GREATEST

A little boy
in a baseball hat.
He stands in the field
with his ball and bat.

He says, "I am the greatest player of them all!"

He puts his bat on his shoulder
and tosses up his ball.

And the ball goes up
and the ball comes down.
He swings his bat
all the way around.

The world is so still
you hear the sound
-the baseball falls
to the ground.

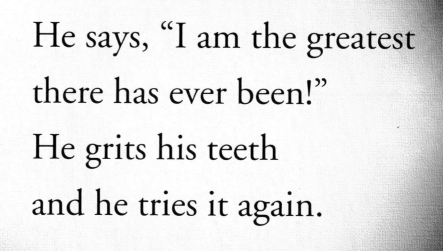

He says, "I am the greatest
there has ever been!"
He grits his teeth
and he tries it again.

And the ball goes up
and the ball comes down.
He swings his bat
all the way around.

The world is so still
you can hear the sound
-the baseball falls
to the ground.

He makes no excuses.
He shows no fear.
He just closes his eyes
and listens to the cheer.

The little boy
he adjusts his hat.
He picks up his ball.
He stares at his bat.

6 7 8 9

0 0 0 0

0 0 0

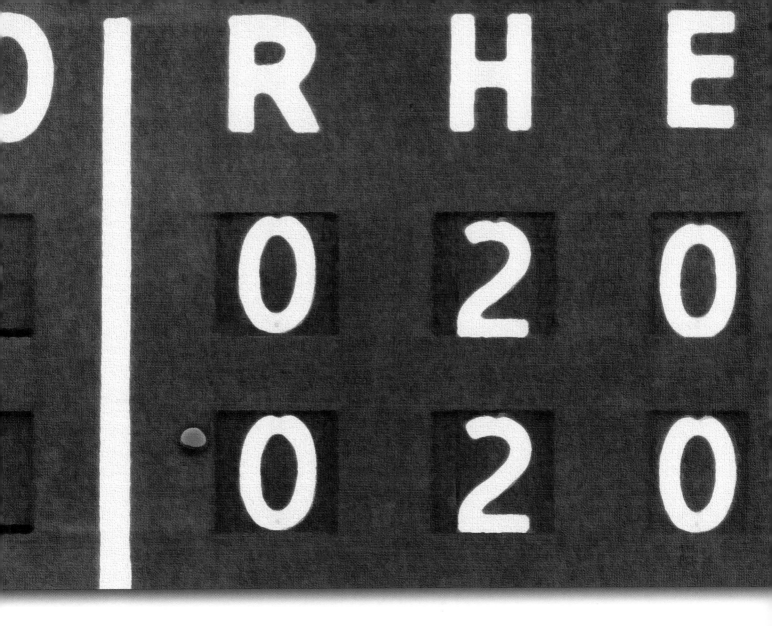

He says, "I am the greatest
when the game is on the line,"
and he gives his all one last time.

And the ball goes up
like the moon so bright.
He swings his bat,
with all his might.

The world is as still as still can be,
the baseball falls, and that's...

STR

Now it's supper time
and his mama calls.
The little boy starts home,
with his bat and ball.

He says,
"I am the greatest, that is understood,
but even I didn't know I could pitch
that good."